Between The Tides

By Fran Hodgkins
Illustrated by Jim Sollers

DOWN EAST BOOKS

CAMDEN, MAINE

Wonder what the curved line in this picture is? Turn to the Story Behind the Story at the end of this book.

Designed by Chilton Creative

Printed in China
5   4   3   2   1

ISBN-10: 0-89272-727-6
ISBN-13: 978-0-89272-727-8

Down East Books
Camden, Maine
A division of Down East Enterprise
Book Orders: 800-685-7962
www.downeastbooks.com

Distributed to the trade by National Book Network, Inc.

Library of Congress Cataloging-in-Publication Data:

Hodgkins, Fran, 1964-
  Between the tides / by Fran Hodgkins ; illustrated by Jim Sollers.
     p. cm.
  ISBN-13: 978-0-89272-727-8 (trade hardcover : alk. paper)
  ISBN-10: 0-89272-727-6
  1. Tide pool animals--Juvenile literature. 2. Tide pool ecol-
ogy--Juvenile literature. I. Sollers, Jim, 1951- ill. II. Title.
  QL122.2.H36676 2007
  591.769'9--dc22
                                              2006035580

The ocean is always moving. Every day, twice a day, the tide comes in and goes out. As the water moves, changes happen. For the animals that live in the tidal zone, sometimes there's plenty of water and sometimes, there's not.

Sea creatures need water. They get food from it, oxygen from it, and some even use it to move. Being left on the shore exposes them to danger from predators, too. How do animals manage if they live in a place that the outgoing tide leaves high and dry twice a day?

It turns out, there are lots of ways.

If you lived where the sea was

and then wasn't,
you could . . .

Keep a little bit of
the sea with you.

(The blue mussel closes its shell tightly when
the sea retreats. Within the shell is a little water.
It's not much, but it's enough for the mussel to get
oxygen from until the sea returns.)

If you lived where the sea was   and then wasn't, you could . . .

Look boring.

(Out of the water, the nudibranch looks like a bit of unappetizing goo. Under water, this amazing little creature reveals its exotic looks, including two sense organs called rhinophores, and a tuft of gills.)

If you lived where the sea was   and then wasn't, you could . . .

Turn yourself outside-in.

(The sea anemone pulls its tentacles inside
when the tide goes out. It has enough water inside
its blobby body to stay alive until the sea returns.)

If you lived where the sea was

and then wasn't, you could . . .

Run for it.

(The crab can move quickly, sometimes fast enough to catch up with the retreating tide. It will come back when the sea returns.)

If you lived where the sea was

and then wasn't,
you could . . .

Hold on tight.

(The periwinkle snail clings to rocks and seaweed with a strong, muscular foot. When the tide goes out, it hunkers down to trap water inside its shell. If it gets pulled off, the periwinkle withdraws, closing its shell tight with a special door called an operculum.)

If you lived where the sea was

and then wasn't, you could . . .

Go underneath.

(The sea worm hides among a mat of mussels, staying wet and out of sight, until the sea returns.)

If you lived where the sea was

and then wasn't, you could . . .

Pick your spot carefully.

(The sea star walks with a water-powered system of tube feet. It cannot move unless it's in water, so it has to make sure it's not caught high and dry. It lives in a deep spot, called a tide pool, which the retreating tide leaves full of water. In a tide pool, a sea star can stay active all during low tide.)

If you lived where the sea was

and then wasn't, you could . . .

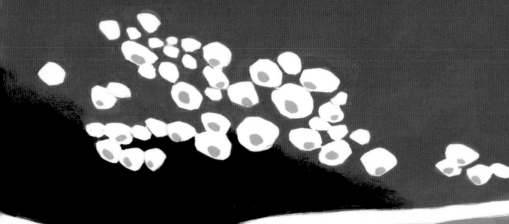

Back up and hide out.

(The young lobster swims backward with strokes
of its tail, and hides under rocks to stay wet.)

If you lived where the sea was

and then wasn't, you could . . .

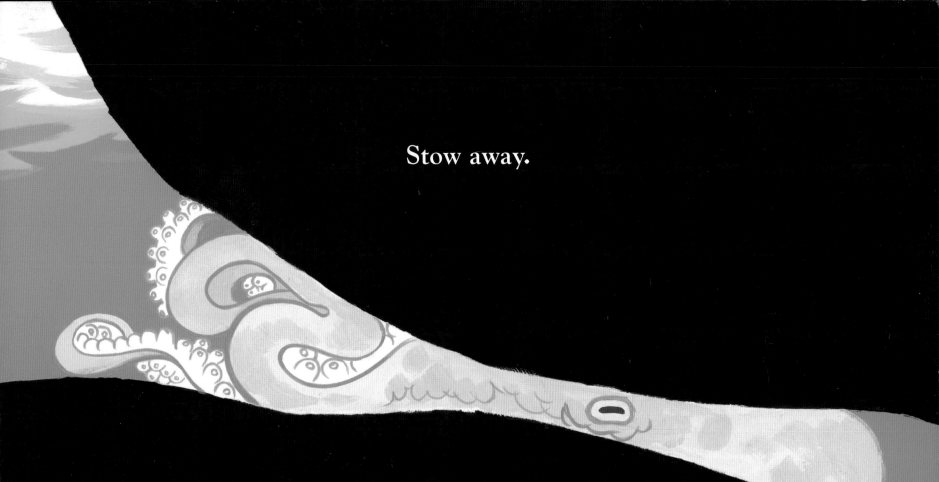

Stow away.

(The octopus has no bones, so it can squeeze into very small places. When the tide goes out, it crawls into a water-filled cave or crevice to await the sea's return.)

If you lived where the sea was

and then wasn't, you could . . .

Furl your tentacles.

(The sea cucumber opens its tentacles under water to catch the tiny particles it eats. When the water recedes, though, it pulls the delicate structures into its body and waits for the water to come back.)

If you lived where the sea was

and then wasn't, you could . . .

Be a prickly customer.

(The sea urchin has spines that make it hard to eat, whether it's above water or below.)

If you lived where the sea was   and then wasn't, you could . . .

Contain yourself.

(The barnacle is like a tiny crab that lives in a shell. Underwater, it reaches out with its legs to catch food. When the tide goes out, the barnacle pulls its legs inside and closes up the shell like a person shutting a door.)

If you lived where the sea was   and then wasn't, you could . . .

Dart and dash.

(The silverside minnow is a little fish with an
almost transparent body that makes it hard to see.
Combined with its speed, this makes the silverside
hard to catch.)

The Story Behind the Story

Every day the animals in this book are covered by sea water
and then, within hours, left high and dry. Why does this happen?
The rise and fall of the ocean's water is called the tide.
The tide happens because the Moon and the Earth
are in a tug-of-war with each other. The Earth is
trying to pull the Moon to Earth, and the Moon
is trying to pull the Earth to the Moon. Neither
Earth nor Moon can ever win this contest. The
Moon's pull affects everything on Earth, but
what we notice most is what the Moon does
to the water in the ocean.

Imagine that two friends wave goodbye at a dock on the seashore. One sails out to sea, while the other stays on the shore. Over the next twelve hours, the sea rises and falls with the tide. The friend on the boat doesn't notice the tide. That's because in the open ocean, the pull of the Moon raises the water just a little, usually only a few inches, especially far out to sea. The friend on the shore notices the tide, though! When the dock and the shore are under the Moon, the Moon pulls the ocean up and up, onto the land. That's what we call high tide.

As time passes the Earth turns, and the dock is no longer under the Moon. The strongest part of the Moon's pull is somewhere else. The water moves back out to sea. We call this low tide.

The difference between high tide and low tide is called the tidal range. It has a high point and a low point. When shown on a graph, the tidal range shows a surprising shape. It makes a curve that looks a lot like a wave. And that's what you see at the beginning and end of this book.